To Cameron
From Mommy & Daddy
Christmas 1979

The Adventures of Nanabush:
Ojibway Indian Stories

Compiled by Emerson Coatsworth
and David Coatsworth
Illustrated by Francis Kagige

Told by Sam Snake,
Chief Elijah Yellowhead,
Alder York, David Simcoe,
Annie King

The Adventures of Nanabush: Ojibway Indian Stories

Doubleday Canada Limited
Toronto

Copyright © 1979 by Doubleday Canada Limited
All rights reserved
cloth ISBN 0-385-14248-X
paper ISBN 0-385-14249-8
Library of Congress catalog card number 79-89499
Manufactured in Canada
Designed by William Rueter

Contents

The Adventures of Nanabush:
Ojibway Indian Stories

How Nanabush Created the World

In the beginning, so the Ojibway story tellers say, the world in which we live did not exist. In its place was a far older world, the home of the first birds and animals, and of the mighty magician, Nanabush.

To look at Nanabush, you would have thought him quite an ordinary sort of man. Unless you had seen him performing his deeds of wonder, you would never have imagined that it was he, and he alone, who created the world we see around us today. So powerful a magician was he, that he could turn himself into an animal, an old tree stump, or a maple leaf – simply by wishing it!

Now in the old world, which existed long before our world, Nanabush and his young brother lived together by the shore of a lake. For company, the two men talked and played with the birds and animals. They were friendly with them all – all, that is, except the treacherous Serpent People, the evil, giant snakes who lived beneath the water and who tried to kill the kindly animals who were Nanabush's friends.

Nanabush and the Serpent People often fought with each other, and it was because of one of these fights that Nanabush made our world.

One winter day, Nanabush's brother was out hunting alone. When he did not come home in the evening, Nanabush thought that perhaps he had lost his way in the woods. The next day the young brother still had not returned, and Nanabush became worried. So he set out to try and find him. He had often warned his brother never to return home across the ice which covered the lake, but rather to walk around the shoreline on solid ground. He now began to fear that his brother had forgotten his warning and that he had been pulled through the ice by the Serpent People and drowned in the icy water below.

Nanabush searched everywhere, but not a trace of his brother could he find. He knew that the worst must have happened: the Serpent People had drowned his brother as he had feared. He set out again, this time to find the Serpents and punish them.

Now the Serpent People were very cunning, and kept themselves well hidden. Nanabush tramped in vain through the woods and across the frozen rivers for days, and weeks, and months. Before he knew it, spring had come.

One day, just as he was approaching a steep hill, he heard a peculiar booming sound.

'What can that be?' he asked himself. 'I must climb the hill and find out.'

When he reached the top, he saw a little lake in the valley below, and there, sunning themselves on the shore, were two Serpents. The booming noise came from the pounding of their giant hearts.

Quietly but swiftly, Nanabush drew his bow and shot an arrow at each Serpent. Though he hit them both, they were still very much alive, for they slithered into the water in the twinkling of an eye and disappeared.

Then a strange thing happened. The water in the little lake began to rise. It rose steadily, soon flooding the whole valley.

'Oho!' exclaimed Nanabush. 'The Serpents know I am hunting them. They are going to try and drown me.'

He climbed the tallest pine tree on the hill, but the water, which by this time had covered the hill, was lapping at his heels. He climbed as quickly as he could, and before long was at the very top of the tree. The water kept on rising and soon reached the level of his chin, but then, strangely, the water began to go down again. It went down as quickly as it had risen, and when it had receded to its old level Nanabush climbed down out of the pine tree.

'They nearly drowned me,' said Nanabush, catching his breath. 'I shall have to be careful, or next time those evil Serpents will certainly kill me.'

He then chopped down a number of trees and made a giant raft, which he left on the top of the hill. Wondering what he should do next, he wandered away through the woods again. He had walked for nearly an hour when suddenly he stopped. He thought he could hear a woman crying. He crept on cautiously, and came to a clearing where an old woman was sitting on a log and, just as he had imagined, she was crying.

'Why are you crying, old woman?'

'Ah, a sad thing thing has happened. That wicked man, Nanabush, has wounded my brothers with his arrows.'

Nanabush knew at once that the old woman was a Serpent Woman in disguise. He also realized that she did not know who he was.

Smiling to himself, he exclaimed, 'That Nanabush must be a rascal! But tell me, what are you going to do?'

'I am gathering herbs to heal their wounds,' she replied. 'I am also gathering basswood bark. We shall twist the bark into a long string and stretch it around the base of the hill. We shall watch the string and if it vibrates, we shall know Nanabush tripped over it. He is hiding somewhere on the hill.'

'Where do the Serpent People live?' he asked next.

'All you have to do is follow this path to the lake,' replied the old woman, pointing the way. 'When you get to the lake, walk right into it. A short distance in, you will find a door. The Serpent People are inside.'

Without saying another word, Nanabush slew the wicked old Serpent Woman and dressed himself in her clothes. He followed the path to the lake and found the door. He opened it and found himself inside a huge lodge – the home of the Serpent People.

Walking along quickly, he soon came upon the two Serpents whom he had wounded, with his arrows still in their bodies. The Serpents were guarded by a group of fierce animals, and Nanabush discovered that one of the Serpents he had wounded was the Chief of all the Serpents. However, the fierce animals thought Nanabush was the old woman, and let him pass.

In another corner, he saw the body of his brother, who had indeed been drowned by the Serpents. In a flash of anger, Nanabush leaped forward and pushed the arrows deeper into the bodies of the two Serpents, killing them instantly.

'Now I have avenged my brother's death!' he shouted. And, before the fierce guardian animals had time to realize what had happened, Nanabush slipped out of the Serpent lodge and raced back to the shore of the lake, running as fast as he could.

When the guardian animals realized what had happened they roared with rage and summoned the rest of the Serpent People, who immediately caused the water in the lake to rise again. But Nanabush heard the movement of the water as it began to rise, and he ran toward the hill where he had hidden his giant raft. As he ran he called loudly to his friends, the birds and animals.

'Come with me, my friends!' he shouted. 'Come to my raft on the hill. The water is rising again, and this time you will drown unless you come with me.'

The birds and animals answered his call not a moment too soon. Just as they reached the giant raft and climbed safely aboard, the water rose over the crest of the hill and set the raft afloat. In a few more minutes the whole world was covered by the surging water. There was not a single thing to be seen on the top of the water except Nanabush and the birds and animals on the raft. Even the highest hills were now lost from sight.

Nanabush and the birds and animals floated around aimlessly on the raft for many days and nights. At first Nanabush thought the water would go down again, but after they had been on the raft a full month he realized that the old world was submerged forever beneath the water and that the wicked Serpent People had drowned with it. Nanabush himself would have to find a way to create a new one.

'Loon!' he called, when he had decided what he should do. 'You are an excellent swimmer. Dive down and bring me a lump of mud in your bill.'

The loon dived into the water and was gone a long time. Presently, he returned.

'I couldn't reach the old world,' he reported sadly. 'It was too far down.'

'Beaver!' called out Nanabush, 'you are a good diver. You try next.'

The beaver dived in and was gone much longer than the loon had been, but he too failed to reach the bottom of the vast ocean.

'Muskrat!' exclaimed Nanabush, 'you must try for us.'

The muskrat dived in and was gone for so long that they were certain he had drowned. Just as they were giving him up for lost, he suddenly appeared on the surface, motionless, floating around as if he were indeed dead.

Nanabush pulled the muskrat onto the raft and revived him. He noticed that the little animal was holding one paw tightly closed. He pried it open – and there were a few tiny, wet particles of sand. The muskrat had reached the old world after all!

Nanabush took the grains of sand and dried them carefully. He fashioned them into a tiny globe, on which he breathed lightly. Then he planted the globe gently on the water beside the raft, and commanded it to grow.

The little ball began to revolve and spin on the water, and soon it started to grow in size. Within a few minutes, it had grown large enough to hold two ants which Nanabush placed on it. The ants made the globe spin faster and grow bigger. In no time at all, it had grown large enough to hold two mice.

Thus it was that the little ball grew and grew. At last, when the moose – the largest of all animals – had climbed onto it and disappeared from sight, Nanabush commanded the globe to stop growing. He himself stepped onto it, and said:

'Here is the new world – a home for all the birds and animals.'

And that, so the Ojibway story tellers say, is how Nanabush created the world in which we live today.

Nanabush and the Birch Tree

If you look closely at a piece of bark from a birch tree, the bark which looks like white paper, you will see that it is covered with small marks that look something like narrow seeds. There are other marks, too, that seem like tiny pictures of birds flying. Now, how did these marks get on the birch bark?

The Ojibway, who used birch bark a great deal to make boxes and baskets, canoes and wigwam covers, believe that Nanabush was responsible, and the story goes like this:

Once, when Nanabush and his grandmother, Nokomis, were travelling together, old Nokomis became very tired, and so they stopped and built a wigwam so that she could rest. While she lay sleeping, Nanabush went into the forest to hunt, and soon spotted two deer. He stalked them and, drawing his mighty bow, shot arrows at each and killed them instantly. He lifted the first deer to his shoulders and carried it back to the wigwam. After he had skinned the animal and dressed the meat, he stored it in what he thought to be a safe spot overhead in the wigwam. He was just setting off to bring back the other deer when Nokomis awoke.

'Where are you going, Nanabush?' she asked.

Nanabush explained, and Nokomis arose from her bed.

'I will come with you,' she said, 'because I am now well rested.'

'Very well,' said Nanabush, 'but I shall have to leave a guard to watch the meat in the wigwam.' He turned, and spying a large, plain birch tree standing by, he commanded it:

'Watch my meat, birch tree. See that no one steals it.'

The birch tree nodded sleepily, for it was a warm summer's day, and Nanabush and his grandmother set off. But the birch tree soon forgot all about Nanabush and fell asleep.

A few minutes later a flock of birds flew overhead, and then, swooping down, flew around the wigwam. When they found the entrance they flew in. In no time at all they had discovered the meat, and set to work eating it. So hungry were they that they ate every speck of it, leaving only the bare bones.

It was some time later that Nanabush and Nokomis returned, carrying the second deer which Nanabush had shot. Imagine their surprise when they found nothing but a small pile of bones upon the wigwam floor. In a great rage, Nanabush rushed out of the lodge and shouted at the birch tree:

'What has happened to our meat? Where has it gone?'

The sound of his voice woke the poor birch tree with a start. He tried to mumble an excuse, but Nanabush knew the birch tree had disobeyed him. He ran to a balsam tree, ripped off a large branch and began to flail the birch.

'You wicked tree!' he shouted. 'I am punishing you for disobeying Nanabush's command.'

Nanabush whipped the tree so hard that the balsam needles came off the branch and stuck into the birch bark. Nanabush dropped the bough and shook the birch tree. The needles fell to the ground, but the marks they had made remained on the birch bark.

Nanabush strode back to his wigwam, and for the first time noticed the flock of birds. Because they had eaten so much they had fallen to the ground in a stupor, and lay there motionless in the shadows.

'Aha!' exclaimed Nanabush, still furious. 'So it was *you* who stole our meat!' Without another word, he picked up the birds and hurled them at the birch tree outside. He threw them with such force that the birds, like the balsam needles, left marks upon the bark before falling to the ground.

'There!' shouted Nanabush to the birch tree. 'That will teach you to disobey Nanabush! Now all the creatures of the forest shall know that you have displeased me, and forever more your descendants shall bear the same marks as you do now.'

And so it is, the Ojibway say, that if you look closely at a piece of birch bark today, you will see the marks left by the balsam needles and the birds.

Nanabush Learns a Lesson

One day, during his travels, Nanabush was walking through a great forest. Hearing a peculiar noise ahead, he stopped and listened. Then he crept slowly closer to see what was causing it.

In a clearing two animals were quarrelling over a large piece of meat that lay on the ground between them.

Nanabush laughed to himself. 'I shall have that meat for my dinner,' he thought. 'It will save me the trouble of hunting for my food.'

He jumped into the clearing, waving his arms and shouting at the top of his voice. The two quarrelling animals were so startled that they turned tail and ran off into the forest just as fast as they could.

Nanabush laughed again as he picked up the meat. He put it on his shoulder and carried it to his camp.

'I shall cook some of the meat now,' he said to himself as he walked along, 'and I shall hide the rest for tomorrow's dinner.'

At his camp, he made a big fire and put half the meat on to roast. He hid the rest in what he thought was a safe spot in his wigwam. He felt so happy that he went off for a walk, singing as he went while he waited for his dinner to cook.

Poor Nanabush! He made so much noise that he attracted the attention of a pack of wolves who were prowling through the woods nearby. The wolves stopped to listen to him singing – and they smelled the roasting meat. So, as quietly as they could, they sneaked to his fire, pulled out the roasting meat and ate it. Then – to make matters worse – they crawled into his wigwam, and ate the raw meat hidden there, too.

When Nanabush came back to his camp to eat his dinner, he was very angry to discover it had been stolen. He ran into his wigwam, and when he saw that the meat he had hidden there had been stolen as well, he was so furious he could have killed the thieves then and there. But, of course, by then the wolves had run away and Nanabush had no idea at all who had stolen his meat.

'It's too late now to do any hunting,' he grumbled. 'I think I shall visit my friend Cock O' The Woods, the Giant Woodpecker. He should be eating soon and perhaps he will invite me to eat with him.'

So the hungry Nanabush walked through the woods to the camp of the Giant Woodpecker, who was an old friend, and the two of them sat down to talk.

Woodpecker seemed to have a lot to say and Nanabush began to think that he wasn't going to eat at all. However, Woodpecker finally got up and said:

'I think we should have some dinner now, Nanabush. What would you like to eat?'

'Oh – anything at all,' replied Nanabush, 'anything at all.'

'Very well, then,' said Woodpecker, 'we'll have raccoon.'

He walked over to a shelf and took down two long, pointed bone pins. Putting one pin by each nostril, he went out the door. He flew up into a pine tree nearby and began to tap the bark with the bone pins. Within a minute, a raccoon came tumbling down from the branches above, and shortly afterward, a second racoon followed it.

Woodpecker roasted the raccoons and the two friends sat down to eat. The meal was delicious, to say the least. At length, Nanabush got up and, thanking Woodpecker for his hospitality, prepared to go back to his own camp. As he passed the shelf, he took a good look at the two bone pins.

'Thank you again for your kindness, Giant Woodpecker,' he said. 'You must come over to my camp one of these days and have dinner with me.'

When Nanabush arrived home, he pulled down his wigwam. He moved it further into the forest, putting it up again right under the branches of a tall pine tree which was just like the one by Woodpecker's wigwam. Then he made himself a pair of pointed pins.

'I shall make my pins of wood,' he thought. 'Bone is too much trouble.'

By and by, Woodpecker came to call on Nanabush. The two friends went inside the wigwam, and sat down to talk. They talked and talked for so long that Woodpecker began to wonder whether or not Nanabush was going to offer him any dinner. There were no signs of food anywhere, and the fire was not lit. Woodpecker finally decided he would go home and cook his own dinner.

'Oh, don't go,' exclaimed Nanabush when he saw his friend getting up, 'please don't go. I was just going to make our dinner. Now tell me – what would you like to eat?'

'Anything at all,' replied Woodpecker politely, 'anything at all, Nanabush.'

Nanabush stood up and reached for his wooden pins.

'We'll have raccoon then,' he said, and he went outside. He pushed the pins right up his nostrils and climbed the pine tree.

Inside, Woodpecker began to laugh quietly to himself.

'Silly old Nanabush,' he chuckled, 'he thinks he can hunt his food the same way we woodpeckers do. He doesn't know it, but using pointed pins is a magic trick, and only a woodpecker can learn the trick. Poor old Nanabush will find this out, and when he does, I'll go and hunt for the raccoons. That will teach him a lesson.'

Meanwhile, Nanabush was very busy up in the branches of the pine tree, tapping on the bark with the two wooden pins. He tapped and tapped and tapped, but the trick did not seem to be working at all for him. There wasn't a sign of a raccoon. But Nanabush was stubborn, and he began to tap all the harder.

Suddenly Woodpecker heard a loud crash. Startled, he ran out of the wigwam, and saw Nanabush lying unconscious on the ground at the foot of the pine tree. Blood was dripping from his nose. Woodpecker propped Nanabush up against the tree and stopped the bleeding. He pulled out the wooden pins and threw them away. He produced his own bone pins and, in no time at all, had tapped two raccoons out of the tree. He put them on the fire to roast, and shook Nanabush until the silly man came to his senses.

'Stupid Nanabush! You have now learned that there are some things which even you can never do. You must never try that trick again – it is a woodpecker secret.'

Nanabush smiled weakly. 'I have learned my lesson, and I thank you for saving my life. As a reward I shall give you a red crest, a crest that all woodpeckers shall wear proudly on their heads forever after.'

Nanabush took the blood which had come from his nose and placed it gently on Woodpecker's headfeathers, thus creating a crest of brilliant red. And this is why, even to this day, all woodpeckers, large and small, wear a red crest on their headfeathers.

Nanabush and the Giant Beaver

There came a time, the Ojibway story tellers say, when Nanabush was at war with Waub-Ameek, the Giant Beaver. Just why they began to quarrel no one really knows, but the fact remains that for many months Nanabush pursued Waub-Ameek all through the north country. He followed his trail from lake to lake, down rushing rivers and across the swampy marshlands. Waub-Ameek was a magician too, and Nanabush soon discovered that he was on the trail of someone who was just as cunning and tireless as he was.

Now at the time our story took place, Nanabush was living with his grandmother, Nokomis. In spite of her age, she was quite able to keep up with the pace set by her grandson, but finally even the two of them became discouraged. They had followed the trail right to the great inland body of water we now know as Lake Superior, and there the trail had petered out. They stood and gazed out over the rippling blue waters, as sad as they could be, for Waub-Ameek had disappeared without a trace.

They had been travelling for so long that they were both very, very tired, and so they decided to build a wigwam and rest. They gathered the poles and stitched together great sheets of birch bark, and soon were living comfortably in their new home. They spent the next few days fishing and basking in the warm sun.

They had been in their new home about a week when it suddenly occurred to Nanabush that the level of the water in the lake was rising. He noticed that rocks along the water's edge, which had been quite visible when they had first arrived, were now several inches under water.

'This is a strange thing,' he said when he mentioned the matter to Nokomis, 'I must find out what is causing the water to rise.'

He began to walk along the shore of the lake, toward the eastern end where the lake narrows at the approach to Lake Huron. As he reached the narrows, Nanabush looked ahead – and stood stock still in surprise! For there, ahead of him, was a freshly built dam of giant proportions, stretching right across the narrows!

'Aha!' Nanabush exclaimed. 'So that is why the water has been rising. Waub-Ameek has built a giant dam. Well, we'll soon fix that!'

He took one more look at the long pile of sticks and rocks and mud which was holding back the waters of Lake Superior, and then ran back to his grandmother.

'Nokomis!' he shouted, 'I've found the trail of Waub-Ameek again! He's dammed up the waters at the head of the lake, and I know he must be hiding somewhere nearby. I want you to sit on his dam and wait for him to appear. I shall walk around the lake, and when I find him, I'll drive him toward you. It may take several days, but you must keep your eyes open. As soon as he knows we've found his trail again, he'll try to escape, so do not let yourself fall asleep.'

Nokomis ran to the dam, taking up a position where she was able to see far down into the waters, while Nanabush began his journey around the shore of the lake. In a few minutes he disappeared from sight and Nokomis was left alone. It was a quiet, lonely sort of day, and Nokomis kept her watch as the hours slowly rolled by. The sun moved down toward the west and finally disappeared. The hours of darkness stretched out, and Nokomis thought they would never end, but the sun finally appeared again in the east, and slowly mounted in the sky. Nokomis began to feel very sleepy, but forced herself to stay awake. The sun set for a second time, and the old woman wondered how she would be able to keep awake a second night. Without knowing it, she began to doze, and her head began to nod.

Suddenly, she sat bolt upright. She had heard a sound of quiet splashing. She jumped to her feet and ran along the top of the dam and there, ahead of her, was the giant form of Waub-Ameek. She raced toward him just as he looked up. In a flash he recognized her, and turned to dive back down into the water, but Nokomis' nimble fingers were too quick for him and she managed to grab his broad, flat tail and hold on to it tightly.

Waub-Ameek struggled mightily, but he could not shake off the fingers of old Nokomis. He flailed the water with all his might, but to no avail. He could not escape. Nokomis called aloud to Nanabush, but there were no sounds in the night save the splashings of Waub-Ameek. She called and called again, but her grandson was probably many miles away. She clung on tightly to Waub-Ameek's tail, hoping against hope that Nanabush would appear and help her pull the giant beaver out onto the land.

Now Waub-Ameek, as we have said, was very cunning. It did not take him long to realize that, although Nokomis had a firm hold on his tail, the old woman did not have the strength to pull him out of the water. He thought for a moment, and a plan of escape came into his mind. He twisted his body around and, with his teeth and his fore paws, began to burrow a hole through the great dam he had built.

It was hard and unpleasant work, but he kept at it doggedly. The hours passed, and in the east, the first faint streaks of light appeared. Then, suddenly, there was a loud gurgling noise and the great dam

quivered. Waub-Ameek had burrowed right through his dam!

The gurgle became louder and turned into a roar. The dam began to tremble, and then shook violently. One instant more and the dam gave way. With a mighty roar the waters rushed through the hole, carrying with them the mass of sticks, great lumps of clay, and mud and boulders.

Fortunately, Nokomis realized what was happening, and despite her weariness, stepped back out of danger. As she did so, Waub-Ameek gave a mighty tug and wrenched his tail from her hands. In an instant, he was free again, and swam far down beneath the surface of the water, where he was carried along by the mighty current.

When the sun rose, Nokomis, feeling sadder than she had for many a day, looked up, vainly hoping that she might catch a glimpse of Waub-Ameek. The giant beaver was now several miles away, but Nokomis beheld a wondrous sight. There, in front of her, in the narrows between the two lakes, the large mass of sticks and clay and mud and boulders had come to rest. They formed a maze of islands, stretching out for miles and miles, further than the eye could see in the narrow channel between Lake Huron and Lake Superior. This chain of islands that came from the great dam of Waub-Ameek is today called the Thirty Thousand Islands.

Poor Nokomis stood, cold and tired in the early morning light, staring at the amazing sight, and did not hear Nanabush approach her. He was panting, as though he had run a great distance. He saw in an instant what had happened.

'Poor Nokomis,' he said tenderly, 'do not worry. No one could hope to hold the tail of Waub-Ameek alone day after day. I was still searching for him when I saw the waters of the lake suddenly drop. I knew what must have happened. Now you must have some sleep – and then we will take up the trail of the Giant Beaver again.'

Nanabush and his grandmother never did catch up with Waub-Ameek again. They found signs of him here and there, and the trail led them along the Great Lakes. They followed the shoreline, past Lake Huron and Lake St. Clair, past Lake Erie and Lake Ontario. They travelled further east than they had ever travelled before, following the mighty St. Lawrence River to its mouth, right to the Atlantic Ocean itself. They stood on the sea shore, and looked out to the east, over the rolling waves of the water that seemed to have no other shore. They were about to turn back and trace their way to their home in the north country when they heard a shout, a shout that seemed to be a war cry of triumph. They looked out over the ocean once again, and there, far out to sea, they saw the head of Waub-Ameek, bobbing above the waves.

Nanabush laughed. He cupped his hands over his mouth and shouted: 'Come back, Waub-Ameek, come back! You are too cunning for me to catch. Let us make peace and let us be friends. I want to have you for a friend.'

And so Waub-Ameek returned to the North country and became the friend of Nanabush and old Nokomis. In his own magic way, Waub-Ameek created the beaver we know today, and taught them how to make dams such as the one he had made at the narrows between Lake Huron and Lake Superior, though of course on a much smaller scale.

Nanabush and the Ducks

One hot summer's morning, as Nanabush was wandering through the woods of the northland, he could feel one of his lazy spells coming on. The mighty magician could work very hard when he wanted to, but somehow the heat of the summer had taken away his energy this day. He was thinking about his dinner, for he was getting hungry, but he felt too lazy to hunt for his food. In his mind he was turning over all sorts of mischievous schemes for getting food without going to the trouble of hunting for it.

He was sauntering along a pleasant valley, where the walking was easy, when suddenly the trees opened out onto a fine sandy beach, the shore of a bright and sparkling little lake. Nanabush walked to the water's edge and knelt down to scoop up fresh water to quench his thirst. Then he went back and sat in the shade of a pine tree, still pondering how he could find an easy dinner. It was so warm that in no time at all he fell asleep.

But he wasn't to sleep for long. The sound of splashing on the lake roused him a few moments later. He sat up and saw a family of ducks. They had been swimming quietly when one of them had spotted Nanabush and sounded the alarm. Nanabush ran to the water's edge and called out:

'Don't go, brother ducks! I won't harm you!'

The foolish ducks stopped and turned around when they heard the mighty magician calling to them in their own language.

'Tell me, my friends,' Nanabush continued, 'are there many ducks living nearby?'

'Why yes,' replied the father of the family, 'our tribe is very plentiful in this lake. Why do you ask?'

'Simply because I have a new song – a new song to dance to – and I know how ducks love to dance.'

'We shall tell our chief your news then. He will be glad to hear it.'

The duck family swam off and Nanabush began to laugh. He knew now where he would find his dinner! Forgetting all about his lazy spell, he busied himself on the beach building a huge wigwam. He worked away for some time, and indeed was just finishing lashing together the frame poles when he heard a duck approaching. He turned and saw the chief of the ducks.

'Well, Nanabush,' exclaimed the chief. 'I hear you have a new song for us to dance to. When are you going to sing it for us?'

'As soon as I finish this special wigwam,' Nanabush replied. 'I will sing my song in here, and you and your tribe may come inside and dance.'

'Very well, Nanabush,' answered the chief as he prepared to swim away. 'All the ducks will be here by the time you've finished your wigwam.'

Nanabush continued to work hard despite the hot sun and, as arranged, the duck tribe arrived just as he was putting the finishing touches to the great dance wigwam.

'Welcome, brothers!' he shouted as the ducks approached. He picked up his great drum. 'Now I want you to swim ashore while I beat my drum and sing. Start to dance when your feet touch the dry ground. Dance right up and into the wigwam where I will be sitting.

But remember – keep your eyes tightly closed so that you can concentrate on the rhythm and the words of my new song!'

Nanabush ran inside his wigwam and began to beat his drum and sing, and the foolish ducks obeyed his instructions. The first group of them came dancing up the beach in single file and entered the wigwam, their eyes tightly closed. As soon as the first duck appeared inside, Nanabush reached out and, grabbing it by the neck, wrung it and threw the duck far inside the great wigwam. At the same time he continued beating his drum with his other hand and singing loudly. The second duck came through the doorway, and Nanabush quickly wrung its neck, too. On the ducks came, and each one, as it entered the wigwam, met with the same fate.

'Faster, faster, brother ducks!' Nanabush called out. 'You are not dancing nearly fast enough for my new song!'

The silly ducks obeyed – that is, all except a little diver duck, who did not trust Nanabush at all. As he danced up the beach, he cautiously opened one eye. He saw Nanabush wringing the neck of the duck that had just entered the wigwam and he was horrified. He stopped and shouted out:

'Stop, brother ducks! Do not go into Nanabush's wigwam! Turn and fly to the water! Nanabush is killing us all!'

The ducks who were still alive opened their eyes. When they saw what had been happening, they cried out in anger and terror. With a great flapping of wings they turned and half-ran and half-flew back to the safety of the water. Nanabush was quick to see what had happened. He ran to the shore to head them off, but he was too late. The live ducks were escaping. In his anger, Nanabush turned to the diver duck who had sounded the warning. The diver duck saw him coming and tried to get away, but Nanabush jumped on him and picked him up in his strong fingers.

'You would spoil Nanabush's dinner, would you, you miserable little duck? I will give you something to remember Nanabush by – you and your descendants for all time to come.' Nanabush dropped the duck and kicked it far out into the lake. In doing so, the duck's legs were swung round behind, so that he was never again able to use them properly. And this, according to the Ojibway, is the reason why, to this day, the diver duck cannot use its legs properly, and that when it wishes to fly, it must rise from the water and not the land.

When the live ducks had gone, Nanabush turned and went back to his wigwam. He had wrung the necks of enough ducks for a good feast, and so he soon forgot his anger. He lit a huge fire on the beach, and when the logs had burned down to glowing coals, he brought the ducks down and placed them carefully among the coals, each with its legs sticking out, so that he could pull the birds out easily when they were cooked.

The sun was still high in the afternoon sky, and Nanabush felt tired from his exertions. He decided he would lie down in the shade of his wigwam and sleep until the ducks were roasted and ready to eat. It wasn't safe to leave the roasting ducks unguarded, and so he told his shoulders to remain alert, and arouse him by twitching if anyone should appear on the scene and try to steal his dinner. Then he settled down to sleep, but his poor shoulders were as tired as the rest of his body after the day's work, and they too, within a few moments, went off to sleep.

It must have been a good hour later when Nanabush awoke. He sat up and remembered the ducks. He patted his stomach and licked his lips. He could hardly wait to begin his feast of roast duck! He ran to the fire, and pulled at the first pair of duck's legs he saw sticking out from the coals. To his surprise, the legs came out quite easily. Then, to his horror, he saw that the rest of the duck was missing! He turned and pulled at another pair of legs – only to find that the rest of that duck had disappeared, too. Nanabush frantically pulled at all the legs he could see, and in every case the ducks had disappeared!

The mighty magician was speechless with anger. Someone had tricked him. Someone had sneaked up while he was asleep, undoubtedly drawn by the delicious smell of the roasting meat, and stolen his dinner – and had then tricked him further by carefully placing the ducks' legs back in the fire.

Nanabush remembered then that he had commanded his shoulders to remain awake and on guard. He spoke to them, asking why they had not warned him. His shoulders sadly confessed that they had been as sleepy as the rest of his body, and that they, too, had dropped off to sleep.

'You are unfaithful and undeserving shoulders,' he cried. 'I will have to punish you, even though it will hurt me.'

Thereupon, he stirred up the fire and lay down beside it, so that the heat and the flames scorched his shoulders. When he could stand the pain no longer, he stood up.

'That will teach you to obey my orders!' he said.

Nanabush began to think about his dinner again, but the pain in his shoulders was so intense that he couldn't collect his thoughts. He walked into the woods to look for food, but he was in such agony that his eyes could hardly see in front of him. His whole body seemed to be on fire. After a few minutes, he could stand it no longer. He turned and ran to the lake, hoping the cool water would ease the pain. As he ran back, he was surprised to notice that many of the bushes were covered with drops of red blood. It was his own blood, which had come from his burned shoulders as he had brushed through the branches. He ran on and sat in the water, and after a while the pain eased and he could think clearly again.

'I have been very foolish indeed today in everything I have done, and it has all happened because of my laziness. But I will see to it that some good comes of this day's adventures. Hereafter, those bushes which have been stained with drops of my blood will be called red willows. My friends the Ojibway will recognize them by their colour, and will be able to use them for medicine.'

And it has been so ever since. Even today the Ojibway find that the red willow's bark has many healing powers and, when they use it, they think back to Nanabush, the mighty magician.

Why People Do Not Live Forever

After Nanabush, the great Ojibway hero, created the world we know today, he did not stop to rest, because he wanted to do many things to help his good friends the birds and animals. For many years he lived alone, travelling hither and yon, and taking part in one adventure after another.

There came a time when Nanabush began to feel restless and unhappy. Although he had done many fine things – often at the command of Gitchi-Manitou, the Great Spirit, as the Ojibway call God the Creator – now he felt dissatisfied, and troubled in his mind.

One night, as Nanabush lay sleeping in his lodge, he heard a voice calling to him. For a while the voice puzzled him, until at length he realized it was Gitchi-Manitou, the Great Spirit, speaking to him.

'In the morning,' the voice said, 'you are to walk to the east until you come to a swift flowing river. Do not hesitate or stop when you come to it, but walk straight across on top of the water. On the far bank, you will find something wonderful waiting for you.'

In the morning, when Nanabush awoke, he remembered instantly what Gitchi-Manitou had said, and he proceeded to carry out the strange instructions. He walked toward the east. He walked all morning, wondering how far away the river might be.

At noon, when the sun was high overhead, he heard the sound of water ahead of him. A few minutes later, he saw the river he was seeking. The water ran so swiftly that Nanabush became terrified at the very sight of it, foaming white as it dashed against the treacherous rocks, with ugly currents and whirlpools that would surely suck him under the surface. He stopped. Then, remembering what the voice of Gitchi-Manitou had said, he looked across the river. There stood a beautiful maiden, smiling, and beckoning him to walk across to her.

Nanabush stepped cautiously into the river, and to his surprise found himself walking safely on its surface. Indeed, the water did not even wet the soles of his moccasins. Quickly he reached the far shore, and the girl spoke.

'I am your wife, Nanabush. Gitchi-Manitou has sent me down to you.'

Nanabush felt great happiness. Now he knew why he had been sad and dissatisfied. He had needed a family of his own, just like his friends the birds and animals, but the reason for his unhappiness had never occurred to him.

Nanabush and his wife settled down by the river where they had met, and built their own lodge. As the years passed, they raised many children who, when they grew up, became the first Ojibway Indians.

But Nanabush's children were not like their father in one respect. When they were grown up, they gradually grew older and older, while he never seemed to age as much as a day. When he had completed all his good works on earth and come through his last adventure, the Great Spirit took him away – far away – into the west, to rule the Land of the Spirits. But Nanabush's children, when they reached old age, died. They were the first true human beings and they could not live forever. Neither could their children nor their childrens' children live forever, any more than we can today. This is so because Nanabush, by hesitating for a moment before crossing the swift, flowing river to meet his wife, had doubted the word of Gitchi-Manitou, the Great Spirit.

Nanabush
and the Turtle

Think of the turtle, who carries his house on his back. The Ojibway say that the turtle was not always so well protected. When Nanabush roamed the earth, the turtle had a soft shell, which gave him very little, if any, protection against larger and stronger animals.

One day, Nanabush was out fishing, but like many fishermen luck was not with him. He could not seem to catch even the tiniest of fish. As he sat wondering where next to try his luck, he saw a turtle, lying on a rock, sunning itself. A minute later an otter appeared and crept along toward the turtle, preparing to spring on it. Fortunately, the turtle heard the otter and ran under cover. He crawled beneath a large piece of bark, and pulled in his feet and head. The otter came by, but there was no sign of the turtle anywhere. After hunting for several minutes, the otter finally gave up the search as hopeless and stalked away.

Nanabush walked over and spoke:

'That was very clever of you, Turtle. Now, if you know so much, perhaps you can tell me where the fish are plentiful, for I am very hungry.'

'Certainly, brother Nanabush,' replied the turtle. 'If you take your spear to that deep pool below the next rapids, you should be able to catch all the fish you need in a very few minutes.'

Nanabush thanked the turtle and followed his directions. The turtle was as good as his word, and in no time at all Nanabush had caught enough for his dinner. He felt very grateful to the turtle, and went back to thank him again.

'Thank you, brother Turtle,' he exclaimed, 'you have done me a fine favour, and I wish to reward you. I notice that you have very little protection against your enemies, so allow me to help you.'

So saying, Nanabush magically transformed the piece of bark under which the turtle had hidden into a hard shell. He placed another shell underneath the turtle, and just as he had done so, he heard a noise.

'Ha!' he exclaimed. 'I hear another otter coming! Lie here and we will soon see if these shells protect you. Do not fear, because I will be nearby in case the otter breaks the shells.'

Nanabush hid behind a tree. The otter crept up and sprang. He caught the turtle – but, try as he might, he could not so much as dent the shell. Finally, angry and disgusted, he crept away. Nanabush came out from behind the tree, laughing.

'There you are, brother Turtle, a fine house that will always protect you from your enemies. Your children and their children's children will also have shells, so people will always know that in your lifetime you did Nanabush a service.'

Nanabush and the Rude Eagle

One day, when Nanabush was travelling, he was not quite sure of where he was. He resolved to ask the first bird or animal he met. As he walked along, he heard the flapping of wings and, looking up, saw an eagle in the sky. He cupped his hands and shouted in the eagle's own language. The eagle looked down at him, but said nothing. In fact, the bird ignored Nanabush completely, and flew on his way.

Nanabush was not to be put off as easily as that!

'H'mm!' he exclaimed, 'I can see that I will have to teach that bird some manners!' Without another word, he used his magic powers to transform himself into an eagle, and within a minute was flying through the air in pursuit of the bad-mannered eagle.

Now Nanabush had changed himself into a giant eagle with powerful wings and a long, cruel beak. The flapping of his wings could be heard for many miles, and he so startled the rude eagle that the eagle turned and flew upward as fast as he could. Nanabush turned upward too, and followed him. They flew through the clouds and emerged into the upper air, where the light of the sun was so bright it dazzled their eyes.

On and on they flew and, as they climbed higher, the air grew warmer and warmer. It soon became uncomfortably hot as they drew nearer and nearer to the sun. The ill-mannered eagle did not dare

to stop, for Nanabush was swiftly gaining on him. Suddenly the frightened eagle faltered, for he had become quite dizzy. He had flown so close to the sun that the soft feathers on top of his head were scorched and burned, leaving his head exposed to the sun's intense heat.

Nanabush closed in on him, forcing him to change his course and fly downward again, back toward the earth. Just before they reached the ground, Nanabush swooped beneath the other eagle and prevented him from landing.

Then he turned and shouted:

'Now you have learned, Eagle, not to turn your back when Nanabush asks you a question. You have been punished and I will not pursue you further. But because you have been rude to Nanabush, you and all your descendants shall never again be able to grow proper feathers on the tops of your heads, so that you will look to other animals and men as if you are bald. And furthermore,' Nanabush added after a moment's thought, 'you shall never set foot on solid ground again in safety. Whenever you land, you shall always be in grave danger of being killed.'

So saying, Nanabush flew away and left the rude eagle in peace.

The Ojibway say that it was because of this adventure that the descendants of this eagle are known as Bald Eagles – eagles that come to rest on solid ground only when it is absolutely necessary.

Nanabush and the Geese

In the last weeks of winter, Nanabush would tire of the snow and the cold winds. He would often say to himself, 'If only summer would hurry up and come – I've had quite enough of the cold weather that Kabibonokka, the ruler of the North Wind, brings us.'

Now in those early days, the Ojibway couldn't do much about the cold weather except to build their wigwam fires higher, and wrap themselves up in thicker blankets of fur. But Nanabush was an unusual man. He sat down and thought of a way to escape from winter.

He did not tell anyone of the great idea which came to him. He kept it a close secret all summer. Then, when the leaves turned, and the first frosts came again, and the other Ojibway were preparing for another winter, Nanabush went out to a wild rice marsh. He waited there until a flight of wild geese came to land, to feed and rest on their annual journey to the warm southland. Nanabush went up to the chief goose, and spoke to him in his own language.

'Ah-neen, great chief of the wild geese, good day to you!' he exclaimed.

The chief looked up, surprised that Nanabush had been able to come so close to him without making a noise. 'Greetings, Nanabush. I hope you have not come to play any of your tricks on us.'

Nanabush looked astonished, and then he laughed. 'Why no, I would not play tricks on such good friends of mine as the wild goose tribe. As a matter of fact, I have come to ask you a favour.'

The chief looked at Nanabush with suspicion. After all, Nanabush might be a fine fellow, and there was no doubt he had done much good, but he was also a trickster. He said nothing, and so Nanabush continued.

'I am not as young as I used to be,' he said, 'and I find these northern winters very hard on me. I long to go down south, south with the birds, where the sun always shines and the winds are warm.'

'But Nanabush,' exclaimed the chief, 'you could not possibly come with us – why – you can't fly!'

'Ah, but this is why I am asking you a favour,' replied Nanabush softly. 'You are chief of a very powerful tribe. Surely, among all of you, you and your birds could carry me down to the southland?'

The chief thought about it, and tried to argue with Nanabush, but the great magician had an answer for every argument. Finally, the chief went off to consult with some of the other geese. In the end, he came back and spoke to Nanabush, who was sitting, waiting patiently, on a fallen log.

'I have spoken to my tribe,' the chief of the wild geese said, 'and we have agreed that between us we will be able to carry you south. However, we will only do this on three conditions. First, there must be no tricks. Second, you must not talk, and third, you mustn't look down. Do you agree?'

'Oh, yes, indeed I agree!' Nanabush answered eagerly. 'I will do exactly as you say.'

'Well, you'd better,' grunted the chief, 'otherwise we will drop you. There must be no tricks while we are in the southland, either.

Otherwise we will leave you there next spring when we return to the northland.'

And so it was settled. That very afternoon, the great flight of wild geese flew off from the wild rice marsh and began the next stage of their long, tiring journey over the northern lakes and forests, south to the land where the sun shines all winter long. Nanabush did exactly as he was told, and he arrived safely. He spent a wonderful winter, visiting the Indians who lived in the south, learning their ways, and telling them of his own exciting adventures in the northland.

When spring came, however, Nanabush was quite ready to return home. He knew the sun would be warm in northern Canada, and he missed his friends, the Ojibway, and the birds and animals. The wild geese, as good as their promise, came to where he was staying, bore him aloft into the upper air, and began the journey north. As they flew, Nanabush grew more and more excited at the prospect of getting home. He had so much to tell his friends about the south that he could hardly wait for the flight to be over.

The wild geese flew on and on. Suddenly, there was a shout from below. 'Look! look! There is Nanabush flying with the wild geese!' someone exclaimed in a loud voice. Nanabush realized with joy that he must almost be home, that he must already be flying over the land of the Ojibway. How soon now would he be home? Where exactly was he? In his excitement he forgot his promise – and he looked down.

Poor Nanabush! Without an instant's warning, the wild geese released him, and he fell – down, down, swiftly down, toward the ground. 'Oh,' groaned the hero to himself, 'what a fool I am! What can I do to save myself, what can I do?'

Before he could think another thought, he came to earth. And suddenly, all was darkness. Nanabush opened his eyes. What had happened? Where was he? Something had broken his fall, something warm and soft, for he could feel it beneath him. He reached out and found he was trapped in a narrow space, with rough woody walls. Where could he be? He tried to scramble up, for he could see the light of day, away above him, but he couldn't budge. He was stuck!

'I may be alive,' Nanabush said out loud, 'but I might just as well be dead, for all the good it is doing me. I can't move a muscle!'

Just as he spoke, there was a loud, rumbling roar beneath him. The whole earth seemed to shake. Nanabush felt himself turning upside down. In an instant, he knew what was happening, and where he was. By luck he had dropped into a hollow tree, high on top of a black bear who had been hibernating there for the winter. The bear had been stunned when Nanabush fell on top of him but, at the sound of his voice, had come to, and had sprung up in an effort to get out of the tree. So strong was the bear that he got above Nanabush and began to climb out of the hollow tree as fast he could. Quickly, Nanabush grabbed the bear's tail, and in just a moment he found himself sitting outside on the ground, rubbing the sunlight from his eyes. The bear had pulled him out and fled into the woods, wondering what on earth had happened to interrupt his winter's sleep.

Nanabush got up, and suddenly he began to laugh. What a story he had to tell his friends! He ran through the woods until he came to the first Ojibway village, where he could tell of his wonderful experiences.

Well, the summer passed, and the Ojibway never tired of Nanabush's strange stories of his flights with the birds. But Nanabush could not get the southland out of his mind, and so, when the first signs of autumn appeared again, he went once more to his friends the wild geese and asked them to take him south a second time. He had to plead with them, for they reminded him that he had broken his promise in the Spring. However, Nanabush was very persuasive

when he wanted to be, and in the end the wild geese relented, and took the mighty magician south with them.

The next spring, just as before, the birds came to where Nanabush was staying, and carried him back to the northland with them. Once again, excitement got the better of Nanabush. He longed to see his friends, and grew more and more impatient. Finally he could not resist the temptation of seeing how the journey was progressing, but the sharp-eyed goose saw him look down and, an instant later, Nanabush was hurtling down, down through space. He closed his eyes, sure that this time his luck would not hold, that this time he would surely be badly injured.

Whumph! Nanabush came to earth! He opened his eyes. He was not hurt at all, but he felt himself sinking into something soft and sticky. He had landed in a bog, a muddy bog, and the force of his fall was sending him down into the mud. He flailed his arms and kicked vigorously. He half crawled, half swam, to keep himself from sinking below the surface.

Once again, luck was with Nanabush. He reached solid earth, and soon was staggering around on dry land. He paused to catch his breath, and then looked at himself. He was covered from head to toe with mud! He ran through the woods, looking for water. He came at last upon an Indian village, and the people, when they saw him, laughed unmercifully. The mighty Nanabush, they cried, covered with mud! What an undignified picture!

When at last they stopped laughing, they directed Nanabush to a large lake nearby. Despite the cold water, Nanbush plunged in and washed himself off thoroughly. When he came out, the Indians of the village took pity on him, and gave him fresh clothes. Nanabush dressed, and then looked out over the lake. The water was muddy, very muddy, as a result of his bath. Nanabush shook his head sadly and said:

'There is so much mud in the water now it will never be clear again. I shall name it Lake Winnipeg, the lake of muddy water.' And thus was the lake named, and the name has been used ever since, though there are probably very few people now who know how it came to be so.

Nanabush Meets Owl and Rabbit

In the winter time Nanabush had to work very hard to stay alive, and the cold, snowy days were spent in an endless search for food and fuel. But when the seasons changed and the forests came back to life, he was often overcome by lazy spells. Late one spring Nanabush had set out on a long, tiring journey away from his homeland. Each day it grew sunnier and warmer, and soon he felt one of his lazy spells coming on.

As he walked, Nanabush began to feel hungry as well. He had been travelling all morning and his thoughts turned to dinner. He went to a stream to spear a fish but, to his surprise, he seemed to have found a river with no fish in it. The truth was, of course, that the fish were feeling the heat, too, and had swum down to the bottom of the stream where the water was cooler. Nanabush decided that he would look for berries. But, alas, the berries grew on bushes on the open rocks, and the sun had caused them to dry up and wither. They were not fit to eat.

'Dear me!' Nanabush exclaimed. 'This is a most difficult place to hunt for any food. I suppose I shall have to find a bees' nest and eat honey.' So saying, Nanabush walked back through the woods until he came to a tree which looked as though it might hold a beehive. He climbed up and looked inside, but the bees were also feeling the hot weather, and they were resting instead of gathering honey. There was no honey at all in the tree, and when the bees discovered that Nanabush was peering down on them, they rose with angry buzzings and drove him away. He slithered down the tree and ran off into the woods as fast as he could.

Now when he was out of harm's way, he realized sadly that he was hungrier than ever, and that he had still found nothing at all to eat.

'I shall have to play a trick on some of the animals, otherwise I won't be eating at all today,' he sighed.

So he sat down on a log and worked out a plan. When he was ready, he jumped up and walked through the forest, calling to all the birds and animals.

'Come, my brothers!' he cried in a loud voice. 'Come to the middle of the woods for a council with Nanabush. I have a new song to teach you.'

Now there were many animals and birds in that part of the woods and, not suspecting trickery, they came as they were bid. Nanabush met them in the middle of the woods.

'Now, brothers, it is important that you sit with your backs to me while I sing a new song of magic. It is a wonderful song, and it will do wonders for you when you have learned it. But you must not watch me while I sing, or else the magic will not work for you when you sing the song yourselves afterwards.'

The simple creatures did exactly as they were told. They sat with their backs to Nanabush, and listened carefully while he sang. One reason they obeyed so willingly was that Owl, whom all the other animals and birds regarded as the wisest of creatures, was also sitting with his back to Nanabush. However, Owl was not always clever, and he looked wise only because his face was set in a grave expression. But Owl was very curious, too, and although he sat with his back to Nanabush, he kept moving his eyes from side to side, hoping he could catch a glimpse of him as he sang.

Though Owl rolled his eyes as far as he could, he could not see what Nanabush was doing. At length his curiosity got the better of him, and he turned his head very, very slightly. His eyes opened wide – and he could hardly believe what he saw. There was Nanabush picking up Rabbit in both hands as if he were going to kill him! Owl let out such a squeal of fear and indignation that all the other birds and animals ran off in all directions, screaming and howling for all they were worth.

This turn of affairs took Nanabush by surprise, and without thinking he raised his arms and stretched them out as if to catch one of the escaping animals. He completely forgot that he was holding Rabbit, and he moved his arms with such speed and strength that he pulled Rabbit out of all proportion. Instead of short ears and four short legs, Rabbit suddenly found himself with two long ears and two long hind legs. But the astonished Rabbit did not stop to think about this. He wiggled and wriggled until he had freed himself, and hopped away into the woods, happy to be alive. It is because of this, the Ojibway say, that ever afterwards the Rabbit tribe has had long ears, long hind legs, and must jump and hop whenever they wish to move from one place to another.

Owl was particularly anxious to get away with the other birds and animals, for it had been he who had warned them of Nanabush's trickery. But Owl was not that lucky. When Rabbit had slithered out of Nanabush's hands, the trickster made a dive for Owl, and when he caught him, fixed his eyes so that they could stare only straight ahead.

'I will teach you to interfere with my plans,' Nanabush told him. 'Forever and forever, all owls will have eyes like yours now. They may look straight ahead, but if they wish to look from side to side, they will have to turn their whole head.'

When the other animals heard what Nanabush had done to Owl, they laughed and laughed at the poor bird's plight. Owl felt so foolish that he hid deep in the woods and only appeared in the evenings when the sun had gone down. And that is why today owls only come out at night.

Why Moss Grows on Rocks

In the northland, the mossy rocks which are such a common sight are also a source of great wonder to the Ojibway. Moss never seems to have soil underneath it, yet there it is, thick and strong, just as though it were growing in rich, black earth. To satisfy the Ojibways' curiosity about how moss grows, their story tellers relate the following story:

Long, long ago, when the mighty magician Nanabush was living on earth, there was no moss. Nanabush had created many things, and he spent a great deal of time helping his friends and making life easier for them. Now Nanabush had several brothers, but unfortunately they were not like him. One of them, indeed, was very lazy. He would not hunt or fish for his food. Instead, he preferred to travel around and persuade Ojibway families to take him in and let him live with them as their guest.

Ojibway families were accustomed to having guests stay with them. It was an easy thing for a hunter to lose his way in the woods, and have to stay overnight at the first lodge he could find – if he were lucky enough to find one. So the custom grew of welcoming strangers, giving them food and a place to sleep. Besides, life could be very lonely in the northern woods, and a stranger could help to pass the time away by telling of his adventures.

Well, Nanabush's lazy brother would take advantage of this hospitality, and he would stay and stay – until people had to ask him to leave, for he never did anything in return for the food and bed he received. Finally, the time came when all the Ojibway knew about this lazy brother, and no one would take him in as a guest. In the end, he travelled to Nanabush's wigwam, knowing that the mighty magician had a kind heart, and would not see him starve.

Nanabush took his brother into his home and, as usual, the lazy man did not appreciate it. He slept late every morning and, when he did get up, he just sat out in the sun if the weather was warm, or inside by the fire if the weather was cold. Nanabush spent his time cooking and hunting, fishing and collecting firewood, but never once did his brother lift a finger to help.

Nanabush was such a clever hunter that soon the animals near his camp came to fear him, for they knew they could not outwit him. As time went by, there were fewer and fewer animals and, finally, the few that were left held a meeting. They decided that Nanabush must be killed, because if he wasn't, he would soon kill and eat them all. They thought of a plan, and called on the bear to carry it out. The bear was to sneak up to Nanabush's wigwam during the night, when the snow lay deep, and then walk away toward a certain lake. Nanabush would see the bear's tracks in the morning and follow them, not realizing that the tracks would lead to the home of an evil spirit who would help them to kill him.

Just as they had planned, Nanabush woke up in the morning and saw the bear tracks in the snow. After breakfast, leaving his lazy brother sitting by the fire, he picked up his bow and arrow and, putting on his snowshoes, set out to follow the bear tracks. It was a long and winding trail, but Nanabush followed it swiftly. The tracks led, finally, out over the frozen surface of a big lake, and disappeared into a peculiar hole in the ice.

Nanabush stared at the hole, wondering where it led. Finally, his curiosity got the better of him and he climbed down into it. He found himself in a tunnel, which led down, down under the bottom of the lake. He walked along, until he found himself in the home of the wicked spirit. There were all the other animals and, as soon as they saw him, they pounced on him, but the wily Nanabush was too quick for them. He raced right through the spirit's home and followed along the tunnel. He ran on for a long, long time, with the wild animals following closely behind him.

Now Nanabush was a wonderful runner, and after an hour or so the animals grew tired and slowed down. Finally, they were forced to stop and catch their breath. But Nanabush kept on running, and an hour later he had put a great distance between the wild animals and himself. He had no idea where he was. He couldn't go back and so he kept on – and on and on. The hours passed, and the hours turned into days. It was lucky indeed that Nanabush was such a mighty magician, for he could go without food or sleep for days at a time. He travelled on, without stopping, and by the time the tunnel came back up to the surface of the ground, he had been underground almost a month. Nanabush began the long journey home, and when at last he reached his camp, almost another month had gone by.

Now, in the meantime, Nanabush's lazy brother had wondered what had happened to him. He sat by the fire all during the first day, and grew angry when Nanabush did not come home at sundown with food for him to eat, or bring in firewood to keep him warm. He grumbled to himself and found a little leftover food to eat. There was some firewood and, grumbling even louder, he carried this in to build up the fire for the night.

The next day he continued to wait, but of course Nanabush did not appear. Another day came and went, and so did the day after. There was no food and no firewood. The lazy brother went outside and called Nanabush. He wandered through the woods, calling and shouting, but the woods were silent.

The days passed, and the lazy brother grew weak from hunger and cold. Finally, he realized that he would have to fend for himself. But, alas, he was so weak that he could not drag dead trees or chop them up for firewood. He tried to hunt, but it had been so long since he had hunted that his skill was gone. Finally, he simply wandered through the woods, half staggering, half stumbling from weakness. In the end he collapsed on a rock by the shore of a lake and died.

When spring came Nanabush found the remains of his lazy brother, and shook his head sadly.

'He was lazy all his life,' he said to himself, 'and now he is paying for his laziness. I only wish everyone could see this, and know the sad end that awaits lazy people who will not work for their living. I will do the next best thing, therefore, and make something that will remind people of the sad death of my lazy brother. From his remains I will cause moss to grow, and all through the northland, from now on, moss will grow on the side of barren rocks.'

This, then, is the story the story tellers relate when children ask them why moss grows on rocks. The children know that guests were always welcome in the wigwams of the Ojibway. But they know, too, that guests should not overstay their welcome, lest they become lazy, and suffer the same fate as Nanabush's brother, who tried so hard to live by the work of other people.

Nanabush and Wolf Go Hunting

One winter, Wolf, another brother of Nanabush, came to live with him. Wolf was a sly and cunning man; that is why he was given his name. There were few people and fewer animals who could ever manage to outwit him.

But, sly and cunning though he was, Wolf was very jealous of Nanabush's magical powers. Even more, he secretly hated his brother, and if the truth were known, he only came to visit him when he had thought out some new scheme to get the better of his brother – or even to kill him. Nanabush knew how treacherous his brother was, but he was confident that his magic powers would save him from any harm. This winter, however, Wolf very nearly got the better of Nanabush.

One bitterly cold day Wolf said:

'Nanabush, we have not had any fresh meat to eat all week. Now if you are willing to come with me, I can lead you to a valley, many miles from here, where we can find all the deer we need to keep us in fresh meat for a month.'

'Very well, Wolf,' replied Nanabush, 'let's go.'

'We must start right away then,' continued Wolf, 'because we have a long journey ahead of us.'

The two brothers started out. The forest was deep in snow, and the wind was blowing hard. They put on all the warm clothes they possessed and set off on their snowshoes.

Wolf led the way. He led Nanabush over high, rocky, windswept hills and down through snowy thickets in the valleys. They walked and walked and walked – until Nanabush noticed with a shock that the sky was beginning to darken. They had been snowshoeing all day.

'We still have a long way to go,' said Wolf, 'but it is so cold and we are getting so tired, that I think we should stop soon and camp for the night.'

They walked until they came to a little hollow, well protected from the wind by trees. They lit a huge fire and gathered enough firewood to last them through the long winter's night. They ate their supper and built a little rack of poles in front of the fire, on which they hung their moccasins to dry. They made their beds on either side of the fire from spruce boughs, and wrapped themselves in warm deerskin robes to keep out the intense cold.

Now, just as soon as Nanabush had gone to sleep, Wolf arose very quietly and moved the drying rack so that Nanabush's moccasins would soon be scorched and burned by the flames of the fire. Then he went back to sleep.

A friendly manitou – or spirit – then came to Nanabush in a dream and told him what had happened. He woke up and moved the drying rack back so that the moccasins would not burn. Nanabush laughed quietly to himself and thought how angry Wolf would be in the morning when he awoke and found the moccasins still fit for use. Then he went back to sleep.

Very early in the morning, however, just as the first gray streaks of light came into the sky, Wolf awoke. He sat up and looked at the moccasins. To his surprise, he saw that both pairs were still in perfect condition – Nanabush's hadn't been scorched or burned at all! In a flash he realized that Nanabush had outwitted him again.

But the cunning Wolf was not to be defeated so easily. He arose without a sound and crept over to the fire. He stirred the coals into a blaze and threw Nanabush's moccasins and snowshoes on top. He stood and watched until they caught on fire. Then he quickly put on his own moccasins and strapped on his snowshoes. Without a sound he crept away into the forest and set off for home. When he was well out of hearing, he began to laugh and sing.

'At last! At last!' he chuckled. 'I have foiled Nanabush. He will never be able to get home now. Even the great Nanabush cannot walk all this distance through the deep snow in his bare feet.' He laughed again.

It wasn't very much later in the morning that Nanabush awoke and sat up. He looked around for Wolf and then, when he couldn't see him, called him by name. There was no answer. The forest was silent, save for the sound of the wind in the trees.

Nanabush looked at the empty drying rack and the fire. Instantly he knew what had happened. He was miles from home, deep in the snow-laden forest – and his moccasins and snowshoes had been burned to ashes in the fire.

But the same friendly manitou, or spirit, who had come to Nanabush in his sleep came to his rescue again, this time causing Nanabush to look around him to a spot just beyond the fire. There lay a huge, round boulder. As Nanabush gazed at it, a wonderful idea came into his head – the only plan by which he could possibly reach home safely.

He got up and kindled the fire into a roaring blaze. He walked over to the boulder, pried it loose with a pole and rolled it over and onto the fire. He built up the fire around it, and sat down beside it to wait.

In an hour, the huge boulder was red hot. Nanabush picked up the pole again and began to roll the stone down into the valley. As the boulder moved, its tremendous heat melted the snow, leaving behind it a warm pathway.

Nanabush walked along this pathway, pushing the boulder ahead of him with the pole. Whenever the stone lost its heat, the wily Nanabush stopped and built another fire underneath and around it. When it was red hot again, he pushed the boulder along the snow-covered ground with his pole, once more following behind in the warm pathway it left in the snow.

Nanabush followed the valleys – the correct, though the longest way – and in three days he arrived home safely. Just as he got there, he saw a great crowd of his friends, who had just been listening to Wolf's story of how he had tricked Nanabush. His friends turned as they heard Nanabush approach, pushing the huge, hot boulder in front of him.

They could hardly believe their eyes. Wolf was so startled and surprised that he packed up his belongings and set out over the hills without saying so much as a word. Nanabush's friends welcomed their hero home, for they loved the mighty magician who had done so much for them in the past. They prepared a feast and rejoiced in his victory over the evil Wolf.

Wolf never came back to live with Nanabush. It was not that he was ashamed of his wicked behaviour, simply that he had finally realized that he could never hope to outwit his powerful brother, Nanabush.

Why the Buffalo Has a Hump

One day, while Nanabush was walking through the tall northern forests, he thought to himself:

'These trees have been my friends and companions all my life. Just for once, however, I would like to be able to see for miles around me with no trees to block my view.'

Nanabush had heard that far to the northwest of his homeland lay the broad plains of the prairies. He decided that he would make the long journey westward to see the flat prairie country for himself. He packed his few belongings, said goodbye to all his friends among the birds and animals and Indians of the northland, and set out for the west.

'I'll be back in a few months,' he told his friends as he left. 'The northland is my home, and I will always return to it while I live on earth.'

For many days he travelled through the forests, over rocky ridges and across many lakes and rivers until he finally came to the edge of the prairie. He stopped to stare. He had heard all about the great western plains, of course, but when he first set eyes upon them he could hardly believe what he saw. The prairie seemed as boundless as the clear sky above. The land stretched out, flat and treeless, for as far as his powerful eyes could see. Even in his imagination he had not thought the prairie to be as wide as he actually found it. Excited by what he saw, Nanabush ran out into the waving grass. Then he heard the sound of someone crying. He stopped and looked around. There was no one in sight, but he heard the sound again. It was a small voice crying, and it seemed to be coming from the ground. Nanabush looked down, and there, almost at his feet, he saw a bird's nest and, inside it, a small mother bird sitting on her eggs.

Nanabush stooped down.

'What is the matter, little bird?' he asked. 'Why are you crying so hard?'

The little bird looked up, startled to see a great man leaning over her nest.

'Who are you?'

'I am Nanabush, the friend of the birds.'

'A friend, you say?' said the little bird. 'We birds who make our nests on the prairie need a friend.'

'Why is that?' asked Nanabush.

'Well, every morning at about this time, the prairie foxes come by, ordering all the birds to get out of the way, and if we don't move quickly when they tell us, we are likely to be trampled to death.'

'What!' exclaimed Nanabush, 'I have never heard of a fox trampling a bird to death.'

'Alas,' sighed the little bird sadly, 'it is not the foxes who run over us, but the buffaloes.'

'Buffaloes? What are buffaloes?' asked Nanabush, who only knew the animals of the forests.

As the little bird began to explain to him that the great, shaggy buffaloes were the chiefs of all the prairie animals, a furious barking arose.

'Who is making that noise?' asked Nanabush, looking up in surprise.

'Just as I've been telling you,' said the little bird.'The foxes are out running, ordering all the birds and small animals to make way for the buffaloes. After the foxes pass by, the great buffaloes will come charging through and hold their races for the day.'

In the distance, Nanabush could see the first of the foxes bounding over the grassy plain. As they came closer, he could hear what they were saying.

'Make way! Make way! The chiefs of the prairies are on their way!'

Then, without any further warning, Nanabush heard the thundering of mighty hooves, and the first of the buffaloes came charging toward them. The buffalo breathed heavily as he moved his huge body so quickly across the plains. Nanabush scooped up the little bird and ran to one side. And not a moment too soon. Following behind the foxes, the buffaloes raced over the spot where the little bird had its nest. When they had passed, Nanabush went to look in the trampled grass for the nest, but all he could see were the hoof marks left behind by the stampeding buffaloes. The nest had been pounded right into the ground.

'Just as I feared,' sighed the little bird. 'That was the third nest I've built this summer. Now I'll have to start all over again.'

When the noise of the thundering buffaloes had passed, Nanabush began to hear cries coming up from the prairie grass in all directions. Many other birds' nests had been trampled and crushed, too.

'Not only do our nests get broken, but many of the birds are killed every day,' said the little bird, and began to cry again.

Nanabush grew very angry.

'This is a terrible thing,' he said in a voice of thunder. 'I will not allow the great buffaloes to trample on the little birds, and I will not allow the foxes to act as their helpers and frighten the birds with their threats.'

Nanabush turned to the poor bird. 'Don't cry,' he said soothingly. 'Tomorrow will be the last day that you need fear for your homes and lives. I have just worked out a plan.'

The next morning, Nanabush came and lay in the tall grass where he thought the foxes and buffaloes would pass by. Then, as soon as he heard the foxes barking, commanding all the birds and little animals to get out of the way, he jumped up, holding in his arms a great stick he had brought with him.

When the foxes saw him, they veered off quickly, wondering who he might be, but afraid of his stick nonetheless. A few seconds later the first of the buffaloes came charging up. The great beast happened to be the chief of all the buffaloes, but he was running so fast that he could not stop or even turn when Nanabush sprang at him. Nanabush hit the chief on the shoulders, and the chief came to a sudden stop.

Until then, buffaloes had always had smooth, flat backs, but the buffalo chief was so afraid that Nanabush would hit him again that when he tried to move away from the mighty magician, he hunched up his back into an enormous hump.

'Shame on you,' raged Nanabush, 'shame on you, you great beast! Do you not realize what you are doing to the little birds and animals of the prairies with these daily races of yours?'

The buffalo looked down at the ground, too ashamed to look at Nanabush.

'From now on, you and all your tribe of buffaloes will be cursed by having humps on your backs, just like the one you have now. Also you will always hang your heads low in shame, just as you are doing now.'

Then Nanabush turned to speak to the foxes, but in their fright they had quickly burrowed holes in the ground, and crawled into them,

hoping Nanabush would not see them. They did not realize that they could not escape from his powerful eyes.

'Hide in holes in the ground, will you?' Nanabush shouted at them. 'Very well, from now on, for what you have done, you shall have to live in those holes you have dug in the ground. They will certainly be cold when the winter comes!'

Thus it was that the buffaloes and foxes came to be as we know them today, all because of what they had done to the little birds and animals of the prairies.

Nanabush and the Porcupine

In the days when Nanabush lived on earth, the porcupine was without quills and, instead, wore a coat of smooth fur, much like his cousin the beaver. Because the porcupine was just as slow moving then as he is today, he lived in great danger of attack by larger and fiercer animals. Nanabush always pitied the poor porcupines, who were friendly toward him and had helped him in one way and another many times.

One time, in his travels, Nanabush saw a porcupine being chased by a bear. The porcupine lumbered off into the woods and disappeared. Nanabush hurried to see if he could help the little animal. He found that the porcupine had crawled under a prickly hawthorn tree, and the bear could not attack him without being badly scratched by the thorns. Soon the bear tired of trying to reach the porcupine, and went off in search of easier game.

'Well, brother Porcupine, at last I know how I can help you in return for the favours you have done me. Stay here a little longer while I go down to the river.'

Nanabush went to the river and, before long, returned with a great armful of wet clay. He daubed the porcupine's back with the clay until he was well covered. Then the mighty magician pulled thorns from the hawthorn tree, peeled them, and stuck them in the clay. The

peeled thorns turned white, and Nanabush, with his magic, turned the clay into skin. Off went the porcupine, as happy as could be – for, thanks to Nanabush, he and his descendants had gained the protection they needed against larger and swifter animals who would otherwise have harmed them.

The Helpful Turtle

In the early days of the great magician, Nanabush called together as many of the birds and animals as he could find, and gave them their duties. He told the beavers to keep themselves busy building dams; he told the bees to make honey; he instructed the woodpecker to make forest music by drumming on the trees; and so it went until every bird and animal had been given his duty – every bird and animal, that is, except the turtle. When Nanabush called the others to his wigwam, Turtle was swimming about far under the surface of a great lake and, of course, being so far down under the water, he had not heard the call. When he came to the surface at last and heard what had happened, do you think he went to Nanabush to find out what his duties would be? Not at all. Instead, he sulked.

'If Nanabush wishes to give duties to me,' he grumbled, 'it's up to him to come and tell them to me. I won't waste my time going to see him.'

And with that, the turtle sank down beneath the surface of the great, deep lake, and went on sulking. He stayed below for many days, and the longer he stayed, the angrier he grew. Finally, he became so angry that when he saw a canoe going by above him, he swam up to it as fast as he could, upset it, and ate the surprised and helpless Indians who had been kneeling inside it and paddling.

After his meal, Turtle felt somewhat better. He sank to the bottom of the lake again, and suddenly realized that he had found a new and tasty food.

'I like these Ojibway,' he said. 'They are very good to eat and, besides, they are Nanabush's friends, and this will be a good way to show him that he can't ignore me!'

So the turtle watched, and every time he saw overhead the shadow of a passing canoe, he swam up, overturned it and ate the helpless Ojibway who were floundering in the water. This evil business went on for several days but, as you might expect, it was not long before Nanabush heard of the strange happenings that were taking the lives of so many of his friends.

'Turtle must be angry with me,' Nanabush guessed to himself, 'and he's taking his revenge by eating my friends. Well, I will soon put a stop to this, and make Turtle do something useful.'

So Nanabush took his bow and quiver of arrows and dived down into the lake. He swam to the spot where he thought Turtle would be hiding. But Turtle, who had heard the splash and seen Nanabush, began to swim away from the mighty magician as fast as he could.

The turtle is a fast swimmer but, alas, this first turtle was not fast enough to escape from Nanabush the magician. Even though he swam as he had never swum before, Nanabush came closer and closer to him. In fright, Turtle swam up to the surface. Nanabush followed, and once his head and shoulders burst up into the air, he threaded an arrow into his bow, took aim, and sent the arrow singing on its way.

Turtle heard the arrow coming, and dived back down into the water as quickly as he could. The arrow missed him but, in diving, the turtle had flung his tail high into the air, shooting a great spray of water into the sky.

Nanabush watched the spray go higher and higher into the sky. Suddenly, he broke into a laugh.

'You can go back down to the bottom of the lake, you silly Turtle,' he exclaimed. 'I believe I've taught you a lesson, and you'll think twice before you try to kill and eat any more innocent Ojibway. Whether you know it or not, you've done your duty. That spray you shot into the air I will turn into thousands of little stars, which will be easily seen, and which Indians will always find useful.'

So, if you look up into the sky on a clear summer night, you will see what Nanabush meant. There is a broad pathway of stars in the sky, a pathway which we call the Milky Way, and which has helped the Indians keep their directions in their wanderings for more years than you can count. And furthermore, the Ojibway story tellers will tell you, the Milky Way is a pathway for birds in Spring and Fall, giving them directions as they fly from north to south or back to the north. Thus it was that the sulky turtle, who had tried to do so much harm, in the end became a helpful turtle.

The Granite Peak

Far, far to the northwest, so far from the Great Lakes that it would take three months to reach by canoe, is a high granite rock. No white man has ever seen it, and there are no Ojibway now living who have seen it either, but the old men among the Ojibway, the story tellers, will assure you that the rock is there, and will tell you that it looks like a man. It was made that way for a purpose, and the story of that purpose is a warning, a warning for men not to wish for impossible things.

In the first years after he had created the world, Nanabush, the great hero and friend of the Indian people, lived with his Indian friends. He helped them in their work, making life easier for them, and sometimes playing jokes on them. But Nanabush, although he never died, felt at last that his strength was failing. While his strength was still with him he made up his mind that he would visit his father.

Now you might wonder how it came to be that Nanabush's father would still be alive, when Nanabush himself had lived for so long. The reason was that his father was Mudjekewis, the West Wind, a spirit and chief of all the wind spirits. His three elder sons controlled the North, the South and the East Winds, and Mudjekewis had promised Nanabush that, one day, he should come and visit him, and Mudjekewis would give him the task of ruling the North-West Wind. Thus it came about that Nanabush left his home in the north woods above the Great Lakes, and journeyed to the north-west where he became Keewaydin, the Spirit of the North-West Wind. He lived happily in his new home with one of his younger granddaughters, who had come with him to see that he was comfortable.

Now it was soon after he had made his great journey that four Ojibway warriors met together in a summer camp by a lake in the northern forests. For the first month of summer, these skilled hunters and warriors rested after the hard winter's work of following the game herds. As they rested, they talked. They boasted of their exploits with the bow and arrow, the fishing spear and the war club. But by and by, as the days passed, they came to admit to each other that they weren't quite as powerful as they wished to be. Each had a secret desire, a wish to be stronger in some particular way, but not one of them had any idea how he could go about gaining this strength.

Finally, a wonderful idea came to them. They would make the long journey to the northwest and visit Nanabush. For was not Nanabush the Ojibways' friend? Surely he would grant their secret wishes. So they started off in their birchbark canoes. They had no idea how far they would have to travel, and it was said that the other Indians, who watched them disappear across the lake, were afraid they would never see the four hunters again. The four men journeyed to the northwest, aiming at a point half way between where the sun sets in the evening and where the north star points at night. The journey was a long and hard three months for the tavellers and, indeed, they were almost on the point of giving up their search before the third month was half over. But soon after that, they began to hear a faint drumming sound. They listened eagerly, for they all knew that Nanabush, when he had been among them, had loved to beat his drum. The sound encouraged them, and they quickened their paddling.

When another week had passed, the drumming had become much louder, and now they thought they could hear a voice, coming very faintly from the same direction as the drumming. A day or two later, the voice grew stronger. They could make out words, and the voice was saying, 'Come, come on, my children.' It was a voice they knew well. It was the voice of Nanabush! Finally, the day came when the voice, which now boomed in their ears, said, 'You have one more day's journey, my children. Tomorrow you will arrive at my lodge.'

The next morning, sure enough, they came around a bend in the river and saw a large clearing on the shore. In the centre of the clearing was a huge wigwam. As they approached, a figure crawled out of the lodge, and it was Nanabush himself. Soon after, a second figure crawled out, a young woman who was very beautiful.

The men beached their canoes, and came ashore. They told Nanabush of their long and difficult journey.

'You must come inside and rest, then,' said Nanabush, 'and we must bring you food to eat.' Nanabush turned to the young woman and spoke quietly to her. 'My granddaughter will make you something to eat,' he explained to the travellers.

They went inside and the young woman picked up a very small clay pot. In it, she placed a few small pieces of bear meat, and covered these with a few berries. She put the pot over the fire to cook. One of the hunters looked at the little pot. It was all he could do not to let his feelings show on his face.

'Surely,' he thought to himself, 'that is not all we are going to get to eat? Why, I could eat everything in that pot in one little mouthful.'

By and by, the dinner was cooked, and the food served out on birchbark plates. To the utter amazement of the hunters, the plates were heaped high with meat and berries – and the little pot was still full to the brim. The hungry men ate and ate. When they had cleaned their plates, they helped themselves to more, but still the pot stayed full. Nanabush laughed again.

'That is my magic cooking pot,' he said. 'It always holds more than we can ever want to eat. Now that you have eaten, I want you to tell me why you are paying me this visit.'

The men leaned back on the wigwam floor after their huge meal. First one spoke:

'I am a mighty warrior,' he said, 'but I know that even the mightiest of warriors can be killed sooner or later by a war club or an arrow. I want to be able to go into battle and know that no weapon will ever kill me.'

'That is a simple enough wish to grant,' replied Nanabush, 'just so long as you remember not to kill defenceless people yourself. Just think of me when you go into battle and your wish will be granted. Then you will never be killed in warfare, and you will live to a ripe old age.'

The second man spoke up:

'I am a mighty hunter,' he said, 'yet I know that in the lean months of winter, when game can be very, very scarce, even the mightiest of hunters can search for days and days and never find game. I would like, at times like that, to be able to call the animals to me, so that the Indians in the camp will never starve to death.'

'That, too, is a simple request for me to grant,' replied Nanabush, 'just so long as you remember not to call animals to you only for the joy of hunting them when you don't need them. Just think of me whenever you need to call in this way, and you will never starve to death in the lean months of winter.'

After this the third man made his request:

'In some ways, I am mightier than my two friends,' he said, 'for I am an excellent hunter and a fearless warrior. I have never been afraid of starving to death or of being killed in battle, but I am a plain man to look at, and none of the young women will have me for a husband. I am very lonely and I want a wife.'

Nanabush thought for a moment and then replied:

'I will be able to grant your wish, too,' he said. 'Now that I have my wigwam and my magic cooking pot, I no longer need my grand-daughter to look after me. If she will marry you, then you may take her back to the land of the Ojibway with you.'

The young girl nodded, for she had taken a liking to the mighty warrior and hunter with the plain looks. Nanabush raised his finger and pointed to the young man.

'Now you must look after my granddaughter well if you hope to keep her. But remember this: on your journey back home you must not speak to her at all. If you say so much as a word, she will return to me. If you are silent until you reach your village, then she will be your faithful wife as long as you live.'

Then the fourth and last young man spoke up:

'I hate the thought of death. I want to live forever.'

Nanabush turned and stared in silence at the young man. Finally he spoke:

'You are indeed a greedy young man. You are asking for something that cannot be granted to any man. You have been wicked in even thinking about such a wish, but I will do what I can for you.'

Nanabush got up and led the way outside the wigwam. He reached out his hand and touched the greedy young man. Instantly, the poor fellow stiffened, and grew to many times his size. A few seconds later, his body hardened into granite and he stood there, unable to move, a tall statue in stone.

The other three young men thanked Nanabush for his favours and began their journey home. All three arrived safely but, alas for the plain-looking hunter, in his excitement he spoke to Nanabush's granddaughter the day before they reached their village, and in a trice she vanished, and could never be found. She had returned to Nanabush.

In the years to come, the mighty hunter and the mighty warrior did many fine and wonderful things for the Ojibway, for they remembered Nanabush's words. And all three young men brought back with them as a warning, for all to hear, the sad story of the fourth young man's greedy wish.

About the Artist

FRANCIS KAGIGE, whose paintings illustrate this book, is an Ojibway Indian from the Wikwemikong Reserve on Manitoulin Island. He loves nature, a love that shines through all his work. Though he had little formal education and no artistic training, he started painting at a very early age. His first show was held in 1963, and since then he has had a number of exhibitions both in Canada and in Europe, and has done murals for a school and for the 'Indians of Canada' Pavilion at Expo 67 in Montreal. He has also provided the illustrations for three books. The rich earthen hues, which give life and colour to the legendary figures that he paints, bring the viewer closer to the nature that the artist so deeply loves.

About
the Authors

This entertaining collection of some of the legends about Nanabush displays the great storytelling talents of the elders of the Rama Ojibway Band: Sam Snake, Chief Elijah Yellowhead, Alder York, David Simcoe and Annie King. Having lived by the old ways of hunting and trapping, these elders were able to blend their experience of the traditional life with their storytelling skills to bring the mischievous Nanabush and his forest world to life once again for all to enjoy.

The task of recording and compiling the legends in English was undertaken in the 1930's by Emerson Coatsworth, a noted historical field researcher and writer, and later completed by his son David, a Canadian film producer. The tales are a faithful translation of the Ojibway legends and remain as true to the oral traditions as possible.